This Annual belongs to:

....

Age:

....

My favourite engines are:

....

....

EGMONT
We bring stories to life

First published in Great Britain in 2015 by Egmont UK Limited
The Yellow Building, 1 Nicholas Road, London W11 4AN

Written by Mara Alperin
Designed by Ant Duke

Thomas the Tank Engine & Friends™

CREATED BY BRITT ALLCROFT
Based on the Railway Series by the Reverend W Awdry
© 2015 Gullane (Thomas) LLC.
Thomas the Tank Engine & Friends and Thomas & Friends are trademarks of Gullane (Thomas) Limited.
Thomas the Tank Engine & Friends and Design is Reg. U.S. Pat. & Tm. Off.

ISBN 978 1 4052 7897 3
60312/2
Printed in Italy

Stay safe online. Any website addresses listed in this book are correct at the time of going to print.
However, Egmont is not responsible for content hosted by third parties. Please be aware that online
content can be subject to change and websites can contain content that is unsuitable for children.
We advise that all children are supervised when using the internet.

Adult supervision is recommended when glue, paint, scissors and sharp points are in use.

Contents

The Steam Team 8

Meet the Engine: Reg 10

Storytime: The Perfect Gift 12

Decorations from Scrap 18

Christmas Colouring 19

Duck in the Water 20

Shadow Match 21

'I Spy' with Spencer 22

Storytime: Thomas and the Emergency Cable 24

Spot and See 28

Jigsaw Jumble 29

Meet the Engine: Marion 30

Storytime: Marion and the Dinosaurs 32

Quiz Time 38

Thomas Poster 39

Very Fast Engines 41

Spot the Difference 42

Treasure Maze 44

Pirate Flag 45

Storytime: Emily Saves the World 46

All Over the World 50

Who's Missing? 51

Meet the Engine: Timothy 52

Storytime: Timothy and the Rainbow Truck 54

Colour Match 60

Sodor Steamworks 61

Silly Sodor 62

Percy's Patterns 64

Goodbye, Gordon! 65

The Lost Treasure Racing Game 66

Answers 68

ALL ABOARD
FOR FRIENDSHIP

THE STEAM TEAM

Thomas the Tank Engine and his friends are all Really Useful Engines on the Island of Sodor.

Thomas

They're 2, they're 4, they're 6, they're 8,

Shunting trucks and hauling freight.

Red and green and brown and blue,

They're the Really Useful Crew.

All with different roles to play,

Round Tidmouth Sheds or far away,

Down the hills and round the bends,

Thomas and his friends.

James

Gordon

Percy

8

Thomas, he's the cheeky one,

James is vain but lots of fun.

Percy pulls the mail on time,

Gordon thunders down the line.

Emily really knows her stuff,

Henry toots and huffs and puffs.

Edward wants to help and share,

Toby, well, let's say, he's square.

Meet the Engine: Reg

Reg is a grappling crane who works at the Scrap Yard. Reg is very happy when the other engines bring him some lovely scrap to sort!

Draw lines to match the scrap.

1

2

3

a

b

c

Who else is a crane?

Cranky

Toby

Duck

Cranes are Really Useful!

Cranes can lift heavy objects, like crates or scrap!

What colour is Reg?

Yellow with black spots

Yellow with black stripes

Clang! Clatter! Bang! Crack!?
The Scrap Yard is a very noisy place! Can you name something that's noisy?

11

Storytime:
The Perfect Gift

It was nearly Christmas on the Island of Sodor, and all the engines were very busy.

Percy worked hard delivering Christmas trees and the extra post. He also had all his regular jobs, such as taking scrap to the Scrap Yard. It wasn't quite as special as carrying Christmas trees, but it was still very important.

"Hello, Reg!" Percy called as he chuffed into the Scrap Yard.

Reg was very happy to see Percy. "What lovely scrap you've brought me!" he said. He couldn't wait to start sorting it!

Percy looked around. The rest of the Island was twinkly and bright, but the Scrap Yard was dark and gloomy.

Percy worried that Reg was missing out on the magic of Christmas!

That afternoon, Percy spoke to Thomas.
"Tidmouth Sheds looks lovely and magical,
but Reg doesn't have any decorations at all.
Not even a bauble!"

"Poor Reg," Thomas agreed. "You should
take him some decorations to cheer up
the Scrap Yard."

Percy found a small Christmas tree for Reg.
He couldn't wait to see Reg's face!

Percy carried the tree all the way to the Scrap Yard. "I've brought you a special gift, Reg," he said.

"Ooh, look, another old tree!" said Reg. "This will make good woodchips."

Before Percy could stop him, Reg picked up the tree and fed it to the wood chipper! **Whirrr! Whirrr!**

"Oh no!" cried Percy. "NOW how will I bring Christmas to the Scrap Yard?"

Percy felt very sad. The whole Island looked lovely and special, but Reg was stuck at the Scrap Yard without any Christmas cheer!

"What's the matter, Percy?" Reg asked.

"I'm sorry, Reg," Percy said. "I wanted to bring you something for Christmas."

But Reg just smiled. "You brought me the best gift of all. More lovely scrap! Do you want to see what I've made?"

Reg showed Percy a big pile of scrap ... in the shape of a giant Christmas tree!

"Wow! Your Christmas tree looks fantastic!" gasped Percy. "I never knew scrap could be beautiful!"

Reg had a gift for Percy, too! It was a Christmas star made from scrap. "Merry Christmas, Percy!" Reg said.

"Thank you, Reg," said Percy. "This is the nicest Christmas decoration ever!"

Decorations from Scrap

You can make your own Christmas decorations, too! Ask an adult to help you with the scissors.

Materials:
2 pieces of coloured paper
Glue
Scissors
Pencil
Decorating material

Step 1: Cut a triangle (roof) out of one piece of paper.
Ask an adult to help you with this!

Step 2: Glue the triangle onto the other piece of paper. You now have a house shape!

Step 3: Decorate your house with paper, sequins, stickers, bows, buttons or glitter.

GLUE

Tip: Tie a piece of string on top, and then you can hang it on your tree!

Christmas Colouring

Use your brightest colours to decorate the Christmas scene!

Can you point to the star?

Duck in the Water

Oh, no! Duck the Great Western Engine is stuck in the water.

Quack! Quack! Can you make a noise like a duck?

How many ducks can you count? 123

Who can go through the water?

Captain

Whiff

Bulstrode

Shadow Match

What a foggy day! Draw lines to match Henry's friends to their shadows.

1 Bertie

2 Duncan

3 Edward

a

b

c

Which line leads Henry home?

1
2

'I Spy' with Spencer

 Be a super spotter! Can you help Spencer find:

 1 red tower

 James

Now find something blue in your home!

1 green tree ✓

1 blue car ✓

Henry ✓

Edward ✓

Storytime:
Thomas and the Emergency Cable

Read the story about Thomas.
When you see a picture, say the word!

Thomas   Annie and Clarabel   man   binoculars

 loves to work on his Branch Line with his

coaches . They pick up so many interesting

passengers! One day, picked up a man with .

"I'm a birdwatcher," said the with .

The  with  rode in all over the

Island. He was looking for a special bird. Then

suddenly, there was a loud alarm. Someone had

pulled the emergency brakes! stopped

very quickly, and all the passengers

got off in a hurry!

"What's happening?" cried . "I pulled

the brakes," said the . "I thought I saw a very

rare bird through my ." But and his

Driver were not happy! "The emergency brakes

are only for real emergencies," said the Driver.

"Not for birds."

"I'm very sorry, " said the . So the

passengers got back into and

chuffed on his way. That afternoon, the looked

through his and saw many birds, but he knew

now not to pull the emergency brakes!

Spot and See

The birdwatcher sees lots of things through his binoculars. Which engines does he see?

Can you make a noise like a bird?

Pretend your hands are binoculars!

What do you see?

This bird thinks Thomas is a tree! Can you find the bird's home?

Jigsaw Jumble

Belle and Flynn make a great
fire-fighting team! Which jigsaw piece
is missing from this picture?

a

b

c

Answers on page 68.

29

Meet the Engine: Marion

Marion is a steam-shovel who works at the
Clay Pits. She loves digging with her shovel,
and is proud of everything she digs up!

Here are some rocks that
Marion dug up. Can you
count how many?

Jack

Alfie

Who else has
a shovel?

Charlie

Answers on page 68.

What colour is Marion?

Green   Orange

Marion likes to play games! What games do you like to play? **?**

Let's play 'Guess what I've got in my shovel?'

Shadow Match
What has Marion dug up?

hammer   Key   gravel

One day, Marion was digging to clear a site for some new sheds. "Have you dug up anything exciting, Marion?" asked Thomas, as he puffed by.

"Not yet," said Marion. "Do you remember when I dug up that dinosaur skeleton? Maybe this time I'll find a treasure chest!"

Just then, Marion's shovel hit something. "What's this?" she cried. But it was just a rusty metal bar.

Thomas continued on his way. He was delivering stones and plants to the Earl at Ulfstead Castle.

At the Castle, Millie and Stephen were waiting for a very important shipment from the Mainland. The Earl was planning a big surprise!

Thomas wondered what the surprise shipment could be.

That night, Marion heard a strange noise.
She looked up and saw ... a dinosaur!
Marion closed her eyes in fright. When she
looked again, the dinosaur was gone.

The next morning, Marion thought it
must have been a bad dream.
"Dinosaurs aren't around anymore,"
she told herself.

A little while later, Marion heard an engine
coming up. She looked to see who it was, but
instead she saw ... more dinosaurs!

"EeeeKKK!" screamed Marion, and she hurried away. She raced towards Ulfstead Castle, crying, "Help! The dinosaurs are chasing me!"

Millie and Stephen looked outside and saw ... dinosaurs! "Hurry, Marion!" gasped Millie. "The **dinosaurs** are still coming!"

"Get inside!" called Stephen. "And raise the drawbridge!"

The engines were all very frightened!

Just then, the Earl came out of his castle. "The shipment has arrived!" he said. "It's my dinosaur statues!"

"**Dinosaur** statues?" asked Marion.

"That must be the Special Delivery!" Millie and Stephen said together.

So Marion crept outside. There was Sampson, carrying **dinosaurs** on his flatbeds.

"Don't be frightened!" the Earl said cheerfully. "The dinosaurs aren't real!"

"I'm building a Dinosaur Park," the Earl explained. "So people can see what these magnificent creatures once looked like."

Then the Earl asked Marion for her help. "Will you keep an eye out for any more dinosaur bones around the Island?"

"Oh yes!" said Marion. She loved digging and was very excited. She couldn't wait to get started!

Quiz Time

Now that you have read
Marion and the Dinosaurs,
see how much you remember about the story!

1 What does Marion love to do?

 a) Sing

 b) Dig

 c) Deliver the post

2 Where does the Earl live?

 a) Ulfstead Castle

 b) Tidmouth Sheds

 c) Brendam Docks

3 What Special Delivery has the Earl ordered for his new park?

 a) Circus clowns

 b) Water slides

 c) Dinosaur statues

Can you **R-O-A-R** like a dinosaur?

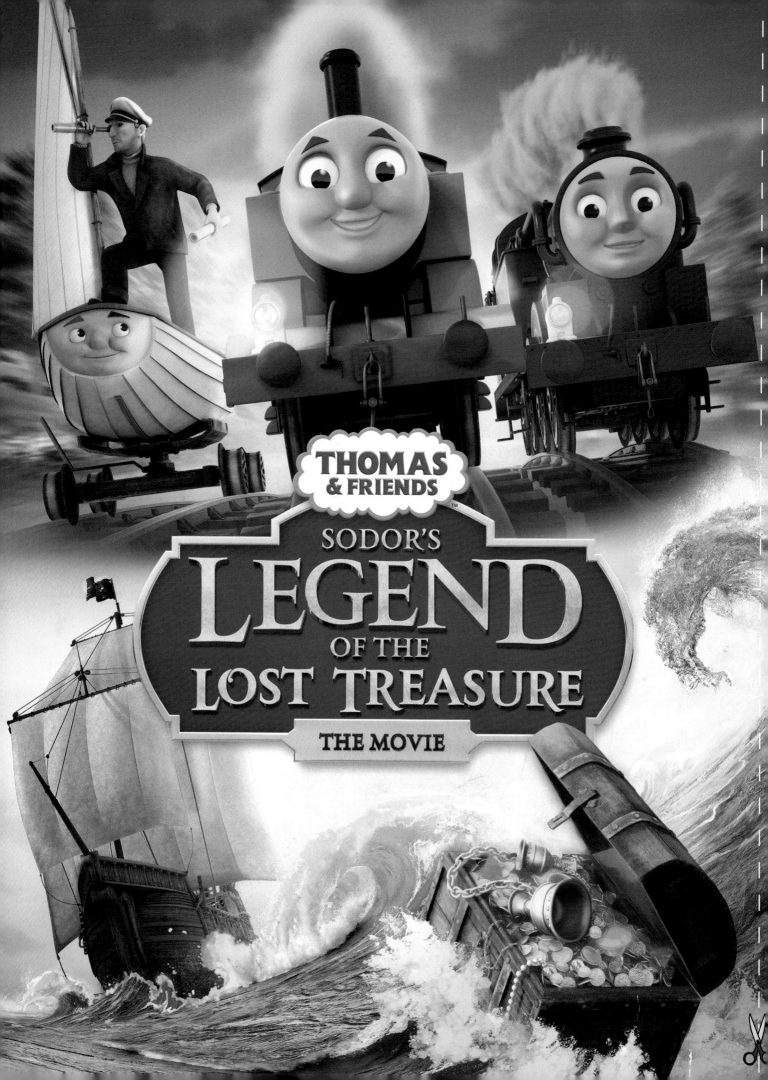

THOMAS & FRIENDS

SODOR'S
LEGEND
OF THE
LOST TREASURE

THE MOVIE

Very Fast Engines

Whoosh! Caitlin and Connor are very fast engines! Race along the track with your finger, and count the crowns along the way.

123

Can you puff like Caitlin and Connor?

There are

5

crowns

Answers on page 68.

Spot the Difference

Answers on page 68.

Cinders and ashes! Thomas is running late. These pictures look the same but there are 5 differences in picture 2.

1

Colour in a stopwatch for each difference you find.

②

Treasure Maze

Can you help Thomas find his way to the treasure?

Start

Finish

Pirate Flag

Connect the dots to draw your own pirate flag.
Then colour it in using your brightest crayons!

Can you say
"Yaaaarrr!"
in your best pirate voice?

Storytime:
Emily Saves the World

Read the story about Emily. When you see
a picture, say the word!

Thomas   Emily   The Fat Controller   world

was very busy. She was hauling sand to Brendam

Docks. Just then, drove by. "Hello, !"

said . "Are you carrying anything exciting today?

One time I delivered a super-sonic jet for !"

 felt very sad. She wished she had something

more exciting to deliver than sand. Then the very

next day, had a Special for . "Bust my

buffers!" said . It was a giant model of the

. Emily was thrilled. She couldn't wait

to show !

But as  crossed over the bridge to find

, the  model came loose and bounced

away! "Oh, no!" cried . She raced after the

, but it rolled all the way to the Docks

and fell in the water with a big

SPLASH! "Look out!" cried .

 and Cranky helped to rescue the .

"Thank you," said . She drove the

the rest of the way to . "Well, , I think

you managed to make that the most

exciting delivery yet!" said 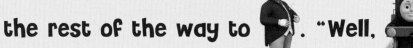.

All Over the World

Can you find these close-ups in the big picture?

Tick the box as you find each one.

What animals can you see in the picture?

Answers on page 68.

Who's Missing?

Which engine is missing from the picture?

Who is your best friend?

Clues:

1 The engine is green.

2 The engine is Engine Number 6.

3 The engine is Thomas' best friend.

✓

Henry

Percy

Edward

Meet the Engine: Timothy

Timothy is a small tank engine who works
at the Sodor China Clay Pits.
He is very friendly and loves being Really Useful!

I burn oil
for fuel!

Trace the oil can
for Timothy.

True or False?
Put a tick next
to the correct
answer!

True False

1 Timothy is green.

2 Timothy works
at the Clay Pits.

3 Timothy burns oil.

Well done!

Trace your finger along the tracks to help
Timothy to get to his friends, Bill and Ben.

Timothy loves to help his friends! How do you help out?

Say, "Welcome home, Timothy!"

53

Bill and Ben loved to play tricks on other engines. One morning, they decided to play a joke on Timothy.

"We've lost a very important rainbow truck," said Bill. "Can you help us find it?"

"It's red, and orange, and yellow, and green, and blue, and indigo, and violet," added Ben.

So Timothy set off to look. He didn't Know it was just a joke!

Timothy saw lots of colours on the Island of Sodor. There were colourful kites, a pretty parrot and even a lady in a rainbow dress. But he couldn't find a rainbow truck.

"Can you help me?" Timothy asked Thomas. "Bill and Ben have lost an important rainbow truck."

Thomas thought Bill and Ben were up to their usual tricks. But Timothy was determined to find the truck!

Then Timothy went down to the Docks. "I'm looking for an important truck," he told Cranky and Salty. "It's all the colours of the rainbow."

Cranky didn't know. But Salty did! He led Timothy to a truck full of rubbish. It was covered in paint splatters – red, and orange, and yellow, and green, and blue, and indigo, and violet!

"Yuck! An old waste truck!" Timothy said sadly. "Thomas was right. Bill and Ben have played a trick on me!"

Then Salty had a very good idea. "If they asked for a rainbow truck, then maybe you SHOULD bring them a rainbow truck! Whether they like it or not."

So Timothy took the old waste truck full of smelly rubbish back to the Clay Pits.

"Hello, Bill! Hi, Ben!" called Timothy. "I've found your truck!"

Bill and Ben were very surprised. "But there is no rainbow truck," said Bill.

"It was just a joke!" said Ben.

Just then, The Fat Controller arrived. "Salty told me Bill and Ben were playing tricks again," he said.

"We're sorry," Bill and Ben said together.

"Your tricks have caused confusion and delay," said The Fat Controller. "Now you are on waste collection duty. Take this rainbow truck back now."

"Yuck," said Bill and Ben.

"I guess we found your rainbow truck after all," laughed Timothy.

Colour Match

There are many colours on the Island of Sodor!

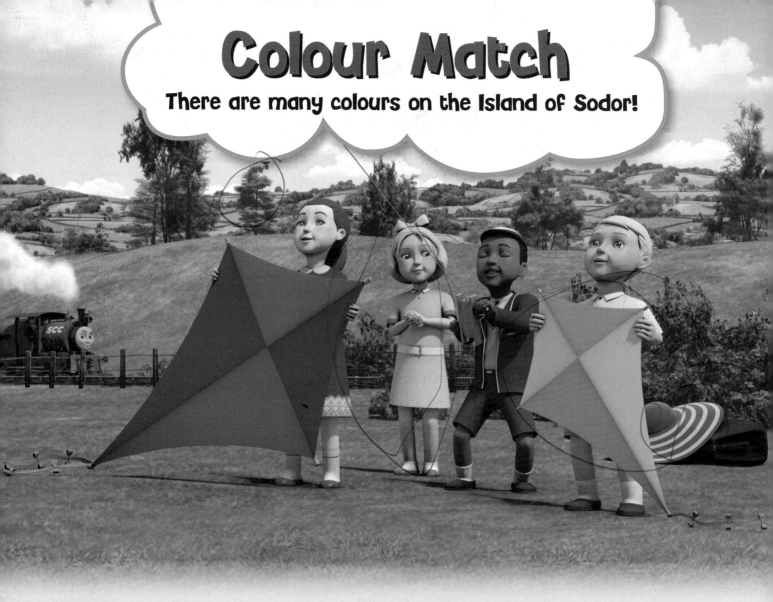

Help Timothy spot the:

green kite

blue hat

red tree

pink dress

Sodor Steamworks

All the engines are very busy at Sodor Steamworks!
Kevin and Victor help the engines get back
on the rails as quickly as possible.

James needs new wheels!
Trace 2 new wheels for him.

Can you point to
Kevin the Crane?

Percy needs a wash!
Colour in the bubbles.

How many men
can you count?

Silly Sodor

Sometimes funny things happen to the Engines on the Island of Sodor!

Gordon has something stuck on his face!

Can you see red trousers or green socks?

Charlie likes to tell jokes to his friends!

What do you call a dog in a bubble bath? A shampoodle!

The Silly Sodor twins **Bill** and **Ben** like to make funny faces!

Can you make a silly face?

James isn't looking where he's going. He drives right into a muddy puddle!

SPLASH!

Henry has to sneeze.

Ahhh-ahhhh-CHOOO!

When the Circus comes to Sodor, there are lots of funny clowns!

Say, "Bless you, Henry!"

What colour is the clown's nose?

What makes YOU laugh?

Oops! Gordon has a moustache painted on his face!

What do you think Gordon might be thinking?

Percy's Patterns

Help Percy complete the patterns!
Which vehicle comes next?

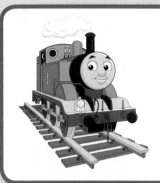   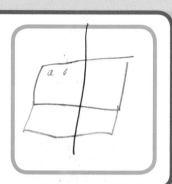

   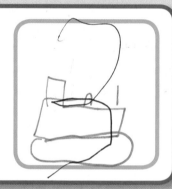

  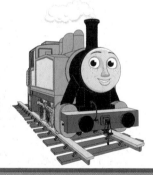 

Now point to all the blue engines you see!

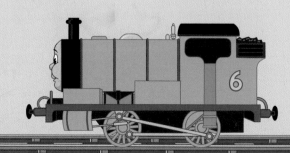

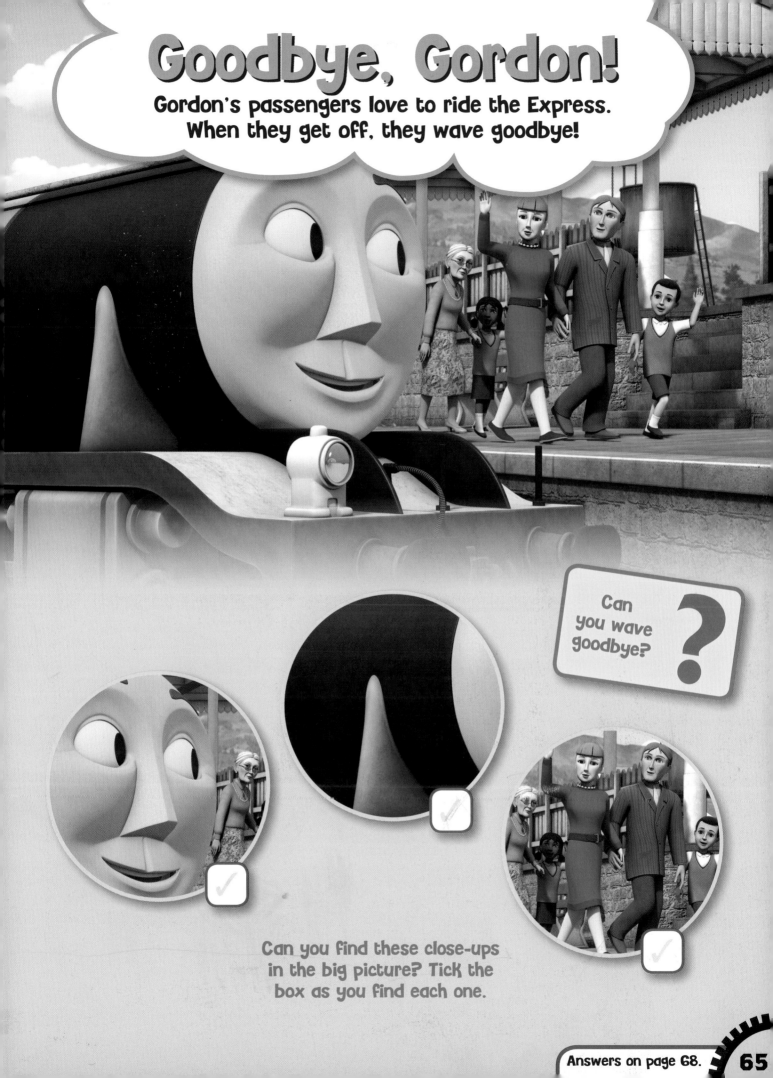

Goodbye, Gordon!

Gordon's passengers love to ride the Express.
When they get off, they wave goodbye!

Can you wave goodbye?

Can you find these close-ups
in the big picture? Tick the
box as you find each one.

Answers on page 68.

THE LOST TREASURE Racing Game

18

Stuck in the Docks.
Throw a 6 to move on.

19

20

Your axles are aching.
Move backwards 1 space.

Finish

17

How to play: You can play this game with a friend. You will need a dice, and a counter each. The first person to roll a 6 starts. Take turns to roll the dice and move your counters. The first person across the finish line wins!

16

You're building up speed.
Zoom forwards 1 space.

15

14

13

12

You've found a shortcut.
Move forwards 2 spaces.

11

Thomas and Ryan are racing to find the lost treasure! Choose who will be Thomas and who will be Ryan, and then get ready to race to the finish!

Start

1 Your Driver is missing! Go back to start.

2

3

4

5 The signal is red. Move backwards 1 space.

6

7

8

9 Yaaar! You're lost. Move backwards 2 spaces.

10

Page 10
1 - b, 2 - c, 3 - a.
Cranky is a crane.
Reg is yellow with black stripes.

Page 20
There are 3 ducks.
Captain and Bulstrode can move through the water.

Page 21
1 Bertie - c, 2 Duncan - a, 3 Edward - b.
Line 2 takes Henry home.

Page 22

Page 28
The man sees Thomas and Toby.
The bird's home is the tree.

Page 29
Jigsaw piece b is missing.

Page 30
There are 5 rocks.
Jack and Alfie have shovels.
Marion is orange.
Marion has dug up a key.

Page 38
1 - b, 2 - a, 3 - c.

Page 41
There are 5 crowns.

Page 42

Page 44

Page 50

Page 51
Percy is missing.

Page 52
1 - false, 2 - true, 3 - true.

Page 60

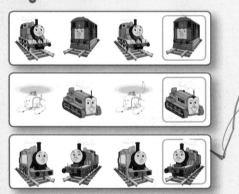

Page 61
There are 6 men.

Page 64

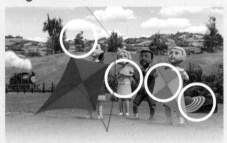

Page 65

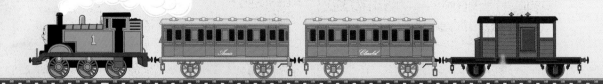